MIGHTY MORPHIN POWER RANGERS THE MOVIE ™

ADVENTURE ON PHAEDOS ™

Adapted by Tony Oliver

Based on the screenplay by John Kamps and Arne Olsen

Now a major motion picture from 20th Century Fox

Book Design: LITCO Marketing
Illustration: Dan Burrus

A TOR® BOOK

Published by Tom Doherty Associates, Inc.
175 Fifth Avenue, New York, N.Y. 10010

This is a work of fiction. All the characters and events portrayed in this book are either fictitious or are used fictitiously.
No part of this publication may be reproduced in whole or in part, or stored in a retrieval system, or transmitted in any form, or by any means, electronic, mechanical, photocopying, recording, or otherwise, without written permission of the publisher.
This book is printed on acid-free paper. Tor® is a registered trademark of Tom Doherty Associates, Inc.
ISBN 0-812-54455-2
Printed in the United States of America

0 9 8 7 6 5 4 3 2 1

Things were not good in Angel Grove. A sinister and dangerous villain named Ivan Ooze had unleashed his power on the city and had taken over the minds of all the adults in town. He had also put Zordon out of commission and destroyed the Power Rangers' Command Center, forcing the Power Rangers to go out into the galaxy in search of new powers.

Alpha directed them to the distant planet of Phaedos, where Zordon had long ago confronted Ivan Ooze and won. With the last bit of power left in the Command Center, the Power Rangers teleported across the cosmos and arrived on the mysterious planet. "Now what?" asked Kimberly. Billy answered, "We need to get to higher ground and get the lay of the land. Maybe then we can figure out which way to go."

eanwhile back on Earth, Ivan Ooze continued to advance his evil plan to take over the world. He was delighted that the Power Rangers were nowhere to be found. Goldar stood by his side. "See, Goldar," gloated Ooze, "it takes true power to make the Power Rangers turn tail and run away. And I've got it!" Goldar shook his ugly head. "But, Evil One, the Power Rangers did not run away – they teleported to a planet called Phaedos. I tracked them there myself."

oze was furious. "Phaedos?! That means they are searching for the Great Power of the Ninjetti. They must not be allowed to find it. Summon the Tengu Warriors!" Almost instantly, the Tengu Warriors appeared. They were giant birds with thick black feathers and huge ugly beaks. They assembled before Ooze, awaiting his instructions. "The Power Rangers must not reach the Temple of the Great Ninjetti Power. You will fly to Phaedos, find the Power Rangers and tear them apart!"

The great birds bowed to Ivan Ooze respectfully and, flapping their great wings, took off for space on their terrible mission of destruction. Ooze was delighted with himself and let loose an evil laugh. "The Power Rangers' days are numbered now. The world shall be mine!"

ack on Phaedos, the Power Rangers were lost and confused. They had been wandering around for hours, looking for something to lead them to the Power they sought. Eventually they found themselves on a rocky beach. The waves crashed loudly into the rocks and sprayed them all with a fine sea mist. "Amazing, the water is salty, just like on Earth," observed Billy.

Kimberly quickly remarked, "Never mind that, Billy, I'm scared. What if we can't find the Power?" Tommy reassured them, "We'll find it. There's got to be something around here that will give us a clue." Suddenly they heard a strange sound. "What's that?" asked Aisha. Rocky ventured a guess, "It sounds like birds."

hen, as if from nowhere, the Tengu Warriors swooped down on the Power Rangers and began to attack. Tommy shouted out a command, "They're after us! Everyone spread out!" Without hesitation, the six teens moved apart and took defensive stances as the birds closed in. One by one, the Power Rangers began to take on the attacking birds, defending themselves with expert martial arts skills.

ut no matter how hard they tried, the Tengus were proving too much for the Power Rangers. It was all they could do to keep from being completely overwhelmed. "They're too powerful!" shouted Adam. "I can't hold them off much longer!" cried Kimberly. It was beginning to look as though the Power Rangers were finished for good.

uddenly, a strange figure rushed onto the scene and began to fight off the Tengu Warriors with fierce abandon. With the grace of a cat and the speed of the wind, the stranger came to the aid of each Power Ranger, sending the birds flying away bruised and beaten.

As the Tengu Warriors disappeared over the horizon, the stranger turned to Tommy and, with a flick of a staff, had him flat on his back, stunned. It was a beautiful woman – a skilled warrior. "Who are you and what are you doing here?" she asked. "I'm Tommy," he replied, "and we're the Power Rangers. Zordon sent us."

The stranger backed off and allowed Tommy to rise to his feet. "Zordon! I haven't heard that name in eons," she said. Billy approached the stranger carefully. "We were sent here in search of the Great Power. Do you know where we can find it?" he asked. The stranger looked carefully into the eyes of each teen and after a moment answered. "If Zordon sent you here, then you must be very special. My name is Dulcea and I shall help you."

ulcea led the Power Rangers to a ruined temple on the cliffs overlooking the sea. There she told them, "The Great Power can be found in a monolith at the far side of the Neola Jungle. The journey is treacherous – you will need the help of the ancient Ninjetti to survive the ordeal."

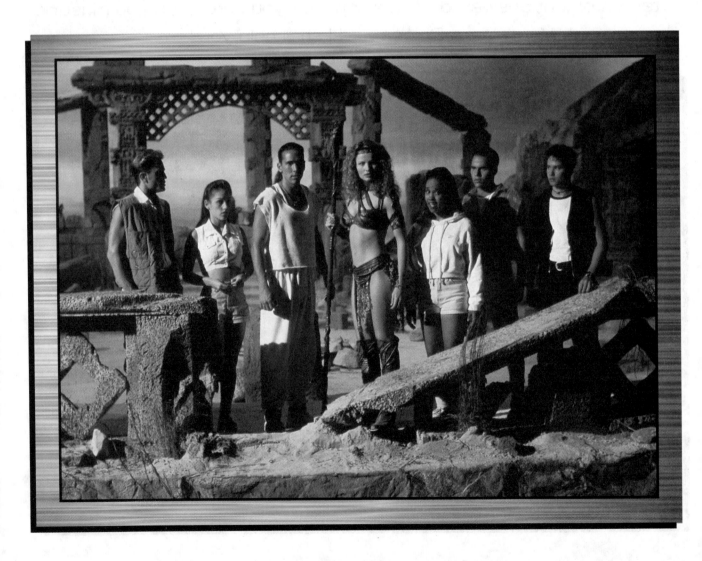

ulcea picked up a handful of sand and blew it in the direction of the Power Rangers. The sand swirled about them as she spoke. "Aisha, you shall be the Bear, fierce and unstoppable. Rocky, you are the mighty Ape. Billy, you shall be the Wolf, cunning and swift. Kimberly, you are the Crane, agile and light as a feather. Adam, you are the Frog, patient and wise. And Tommy, you are the Falcon, Lord of the Skies."

s she finished speaking, the sand stopped swirling. The Power Rangers now realized that they had been transformed. They wore the colorful outfits of the great Ninjetti Warriors with their spirit animals emblazoned in gold on their chests. The Power Rangers were amazed. Dulcea pointed toward the jungle. "Go now, follow the path from the stream and you shall find what you seek. I cannot go with you. This is for you to do together."

Kimberly looked concerned. "But once we find the Great Power, how do we get back to Earth?" she asked. Dulcea smiled, "For those who follow the spirit of the Ninjetti and have touched the Great Power, anything is possible. You will know what to do when the time comes." And with that, Dulcea raised her staff, transformed into a beautiful bird and flew off into the sky.

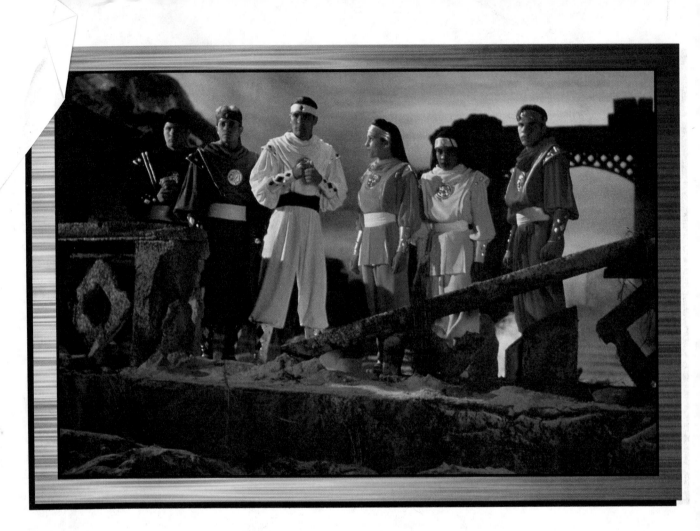

The Power Rangers looked at each other with a mixture of fear and excitement. Tommy looked off in the direction of the path. "Looks like we're on our own again," he said. "We'd better get going." One by one, the Power Rangers started down the path that led to the stream and the jungle beyond – each of them wondering what dangers they would have to face before their quest was finished.

t took quite a while for the Power Rangers to find their way through the jungle. They had to climb steep embankments and trudge through miles of vast swampland. Finally, they arrived. They stepped out of the dense jungle and into a clearing. In front of them was a sheer rock cliff which surrounded a huge stone entrance to a hidden temple. Four ugly gargoyles guarded the door.

Tommy smiled. "Looks like this is the place." The group started to approach the door. Suddenly the walls of the temple began to glow and the four gargoyles came to life! They jumped off the doors and began to threaten the Power Rangers. "We can't let them stop us now. We've come too far," said Kimberly. "Right!" shouted Tommy. "Let's do it!" The battle was on.

The six teens split up in separate directions. Tommy and Aisha shouted, "Ninjetti!" and headed straight for one of the gargoyles while Kimberly and Billy went after another. Rocky led the other gargoyle on a chase up the side of the cliff. Using all of their newfound Ninjetti Power, they fought brilliantly and defeated the gargoyles.

"We did it!" shouted Rocky. "Yeah," replied Adam, "but now what?" Before he could finish talking, the door seal of the temple began to glow as a chorus of strange sounds began to surround them. They were bathed in a golden glow as the monolith revealed itself to them. The Power Rangers waited for the Power to be given to them, but nothing happened.

W hat's the matter?" asked Aisha. "What's it waiting for?" Kimberly spoke up. "Wait a minute. Dulcea said we had to do this together." "So," Tommy continued, "let's come together." With that, the Power Rangers stood side by side. One by one, they called out the names of their animals – Bear, Ape, Frog, Crane, Wolf, and Falcon. The light from the monolith grew and engulfed the six.

The Power Rangers emerged from the light and morphed into their fighting suits. "We've got the Power!" shouted Tommy. "Morphers are online!" added Billy. The Power Rangers were back and ready to return to Earth and save it. They had struggled down a difficult path and had overcome many obstacles to find the Power. Now it was time to go home, where their greatest challenge was yet to come.